A WOODLAND MYSTERY

The Mall Mystery

A WOODLAND MYSTERY
By Irene Schultz

To the police officers, who help raise children
and keep them safe

The Mall Mystery
©2000 Wright Group Publishing Inc.
Text by Irene Schultz
Cover illustration by Meg Aubrey
Cameo illustrations by Taylor Bruce
Interior illustrations by Tom Sperling and Adam Weiskind

Woodland Mysteries™
© Wright Group Publishing, Inc.

The Wright Group
19201 120th Avenue NE
Bothell, WA   98011
www.WrightGroup.com

Printed in the United States of America

10   9   8   7   6   5   4   3   2   1

ISBN: 0-322-01957-5
ISBN: 0-322-02370-X (6-pack)

What family solves mysteries ... has adventures all over the world ... and loves oatmeal cookies?
It's the Woodlanders!

Sammy Westburg (10 years old)
His sister Kathy Westburg (13)
His brother Bill Westburg (14)
His best friend Dave Briggs (16)
His best grown-up friend Mrs. Tandy
And Mop, their little dog!

The children all lost their parents, but with Mrs. Tandy have made their own family.

Why are they called the Woodlanders? Because they live in a big house in the Bluff Lake woods. On Woodland Street!

Together they find fun, mystery, and adventure. What are they up to now?

Read on!

Meet the Woodlanders!

Sammy Westburg
Sammy is a ten-year-old wonder! He's big for his fifth-grade class, and big-mouthed, too. He has wild hair and makes awful spider faces. Even so, you can't help liking him.

Bill Westburg
Bill, fourteen, is friendly and strong, and only one inch taller than his brother Sammy. He loves Sammy, but pokes him to make him be quiet! He's in junior high.

Kathy Westburg
Kathy, thirteen, is small, shy, and smart. She wants to be a doctor someday! She loves to be with Dave, and her brothers kid her about it. She's in junior high, too.

Dave Briggs

Dave, sixteen, is tall and blond. He can't walk, so he uses a wheelchair and drives a special car. He likes coaching high-school sports, solving mysteries, and reading. And Kathy!

Mrs. Tandy

Sometimes the kids call her Mrs. T. She's Becky Tandy, their tall, thin, caring friend. She's always ready for a new adventure, and for making cookies!

Mop

Mop is the family's little tan dog. Sometimes they have to leave him behind with friends. But he'd much rather be running after Sammy.

Table of Contents

Chapter 1:
What Should We Do Today?

"Will you look at that!   It reads twelve below zero out there."

Ten-year-old Sammy Westburg stood at the kitchen window.

His sister, Kathy, thirteen, said, "There's a big wind, too. This is dangerous weather to be out in.

"Your ears and nose could get frostbite in a minute when it's this cold."

Sammy said, "You worry too much, Kathy."

He hung a dishtowel over his head and said, "I'll wear this hat, Kathy."

Kathy laughed. "If you wear THAT hat, you are going to be very cold."

Mrs. Tandy smiled. "And what would we use on the dishes?"

Mrs. Tandy took five big bowls from a cupboard.

They were almost as big as mixing bowls.

She said, "This is a day for hot cereal.

"Sammy, why don't you run and tell Dave and Bill to hurry. I'm going to fill our bowls."

Sammy trotted down the hall. The Woodlanders' little tan dog, Mop, ran along nipping at his heels.

Sammy's brother, Bill, fourteen, lay on his back in bed. He was sound asleep and snoring.

Sixteen-year-old Dave Briggs was already up. He had pulled himself into his wheelchair. He was already dressed.

Just then, three AWFUL snores came out of Bill's mouth.

Sammy whispered, "Good grief! He sounds like a broken snow blower! How do you fall asleep at night in the same room?"

Dave whispered back, "It's lucky I love to read.

"I read until my eyes won't stay open. My ears close up at the same time."

Suddenly, Bill gave a snore so loud he shot out of bed, wide awake.

He gasped, "What was that!"

Sammy laughed. "It was you! Get up, Pig-Snorter. It's eight o'clock.

"Mrs. Tandy made hot cereal for us. But I'll tell her to make YOU some hog slops."

Sammy dashed out, chanting:
"Can't catch a rabbit,
Can't catch a flea,
Can't catch a monkey, and you
CAN'T CATCH ME!"

The two older boys chased him all the way to the kitchen.

Sammy hid behind Mrs. Tandy. He begged her, "Save me! Save me! A wild snort pig is after me!"

Bill laughed and sat down at the kitchen table.

Dave wheeled over to look out the window. He exclaimed, "Wow! Is our thermometer broken?

"If it isn't, we'd better plan to stay inside today."

Sammy said, "The thermometer isn't broken. It's just caught COLD. Get it?"

He laughed. The others all groaned.

Then he said, "Dave, what do you mean, stay inside?

"That's a stinky idea! We can go out, like always.

"We just have to dress warmer. We could ice skate ...

"Or go sledding in the ravine.

"Or see who can find the biggest icicle."

5

Bill said, "I vote we stay in and play board games.

"Or we could have a chess contest."

Dave said, "Or let's draw. Or work in the basement on the train set."

Mrs. Tandy said, "Or how about this? We could go to the mall!

"I read in the paper that there's a special display that starts today."

Sammy said, "You're not going to trick ME into staying inside."

Bill said, "Sammy, just look at the way the trees are bending from the wind. It's colder out there than inside our freezer.

"Don't be a birdbrain."

Sammy said, "Oh yeah? Well, ...

I'm rubber and you're glue.

Everything you say

Bounces off of me

And sticks to you!

So you're the birdbrain."

Then he crossed his arms and stuck out his tongue so hard it hurt.

Mrs. Tandy said, "Well, right now Mop needs someone to walk him."

Bill said, "I can get dressed in a minute. I'll take him out."

Sammy said, "No, I'll do it. I'm not afraid of a little wind, like SOME people."

He pulled on his socks and shoes and coat and hat and mittens.

He called, "Come on, Mop. Let's show these scaredy-cats."

Sammy grabbed a little T-shirt he'd bought at a house sale.

He pulled it over the poor dog's head.

Then he stuffed Mop's front paws through the arm holes.

He clipped a leash onto Mop's collar and dragged Mop out the door.

In a few minutes, the others had the table set.

Mrs. Tandy said, "We might as well go ahead and eat. Sammy sounded like he wanted to stay outside a while."

She finished setting the last bowl of hot cereal on the table.

But at that very moment, the kitchen door flew open.

In rushed Sammy. He was holding Mop like a baby in his arms.

He shouted, "You will never guess what HAPPENED just now! Mop and I almost got KILLED!"

Chapter 2:
Why Didn't You Tell Me?

Sammy's face was bright red.

He yelled, "Why didn't you guys tell me it was so cold?

"I almost froze to death. And my pants are torn. And wait till you hear what happened.

"A dog bit me on the ankle. What if he has rabies?"

Dave took Mop from Sammy's arms.

Bill took Sammy's coat.

Kathy held her hands over Sammy's icy ears.

She said, "We tried to tell you, Sammy. Here. Sit down and eat some cereal. It will help warm you up."

Kathy lifted Sammy's pant leg. She looked at his ankle.

"It's red, but the skin isn't broken, Sammy. You don't have to be afraid of rabies. It's a good thing your socks are so thick."

Mrs. Tandy said, "What happened, honey?"

Sammy said, "We got as far as the corner when Mop's feet began to hurt.

"He slowed down. I guess the road salt burned his paws."

Dave said, "I heard the salt trucks all last night. The salt must be down pretty thick. Sidewalks and streets both."

Sammy said, "Well, then he tried walking on just three paws to get away from the salt.

"Then he tried walking on two paws ...

"And of course, he fell on his belly.

"Then he rolled over on his back with his feet in the air."

Kathy said, "I'd better wash his paws

11

right now ... to get that salt off." She started running warm water into a pan.

Sammy said, "Now here's the part where we almost got killed.

"You know that mean fox terrier down the block? The dog that hides, and then barks his brains out when you walk past?

"You know, the one with the long leash that ends right at the sidewalk?

"He's always jumping at people and getting jerked back by that leash.

"Well, I think the leash has made him crazy.

"Somehow today he got off his leash.

"The first thing I knew, he was shooting up the street at us like a rocket.

"He curled his lips back and his teeth looked terrible.

"He tried to grab Mop. He kept circling us, like a shark getting ready to attack.

"I kept turning around to stay between Mop and him.

"Finally, he ran around me and tried for Mop's neck.

"So I grabbed up Mop. And I ran like crazy.

Mrs. Tandy said, "Did that get rid of him?"

Sammy said, "NO! That's when he tried to kill ME!

"Didn't you hear me? I was yelling my lungs out."

Kathy said, "You know we'd have come if we'd heard you, Sammy!"

Sammy said, "Well, then I held Mop up in the air ... and RAN for my life!

"But that rotten dog followed me right up our porch steps. He kept biting at my legs.

"And my ears were freezing.

"And my lungs still sting.

"And my nose is froze.

"So I'm DONE with playing outside. I've got a great idea. Let's do something indoors. I'm glad I thought of that."

Bill said, "Hey, Dave thought of that! Remember, you said it was a stinky idea."

Sammy grinned and said, "Sorry about that, Dave. But I should get credit for something. After all, I just saved Mop's life."

Dave said, "OK. You get credit for being the hero of the day.

"Now, do you want to hear the indoor list I made?"

Mrs. Tandy said, "Before you read it, Dave, here's the newspaper story about the mall.

"It says they have a display to show our state's history ...

with Native American objects

... and pioneer tools.

"They have life-size models of dinosaurs from our country's pre-history and dinosaur models that move.

" ... And they have a priceless original journal written by an early dinosaur fossil hunter. It has all his notes and drawings.

" ... And they have a diorama of a dinosaur dig." She said it this way: die-uh-RAM-uh.

Dave said, "That settles it for me! I vote we go to the mall." The others chose the mall, too.

Sammy said, "OK, I'll check Mop's water bowl. Mrs. T, put the milk back in the refrigerator and lock the back door.

"Bill, get dressed; and Dave and Kathy, load the dishwasher."

Bill said, "Just a little minute, Sammy. How come you're bossing us all around?"

Sammy said, "Dave said I'm the hero of the day, didn't he?

"You heard him. That makes me the big boss.

"Why else would it be good to be a hero?

"Now, everybody, get dressed for outside, and dress warm!"

Ten minutes later, they were loaded into Dave's station wagon. It had hand controls that allowed him to drive it.

Dave began singing,

"A dinosaur is merrier
Than a crazy terrier."

Bill made up,
   "A terrier
   Is hairier."
Sammy added,
   "A terrier
   ... Is scarier."
Mrs. Tandy chanted,
   "And you should build a barrier."
Then Kathy finished with,
   " ... If he's a rabies carrier."
Everyone burst out laughing.

They made up silly songs all the way to the mall.

"Looks like we're going to have a silly day," Mrs. Tandy said. Everyone agreed.

They didn't know how serious the rest of the day would be.

Chapter 3:
False Alarm

The mall parking lot was already filling up.

Mrs. Tandy said, "The grand opening of the display is at nine-thirty."

The Woodlanders raced through the outer doors.

They discovered that the inner doors were still closed and locked. A large crowd was waiting between the two sets of doors.

Sammy said, "Wow! There are so many people here. I can't move my arms.

"Oops, was that your toe, Mrs. T? I'm really sorry."

Dave said, "Look, now they're opening the inner doors."

Sammy said, "Dinosaurs, here we come."

The Woodlanders hurried with the crowd to a two-story-high dinosaur.

A smaller dinosaur stood on the floor at its feet. It looked as if the large dinosaur was just about to attack the smaller dinosaur.

Sammy saw a sign near them. He read

the word on the sign. "Tie-ran-oh-SORE-us-wrecks."

Kathy said, "Look out, Sammy. That Tyrannosaurus looks so real, it's scary."

Dave said, "Wait until the power is turned on. Then all the dinosaurs on display will move and roar."

21

Sammy said, "Ha! Who's afraid of fake dinosaurs? Superhero Sammy is here to protect you."

Just then a loudspeaker boomed:

"ALL GUARDS! REPORT TO THE FRONT OFFICE. A CHILD IS LOST."

People in the crowd began talking about the announcement. But in a second, the talk was drowned out.

The power switch had been turned on. Roars filled the air.

Children yelled, and laughed ... and some began to cry.

The Tyrannosaurus rex in front of the family clawed the air. He waved his thick neck.

His giant mouth opened in a terrible grin.

His pointed teeth shone against blood-colored gums.

Then suddenly his eyes looked downward, RIGHT AT SAMMY!

Sammy fell backward and landed against Bill.

Bill caught him. He said, "Wait! Aren't you the superhero who was going to protect US?"

Sammy said, "Listen, dino-mouth! I'm not afraid. I tripped."

Just the same, he held tightly onto Bill's arm.

Dave said, "Tyrannosaurus rex was the tyrant king, all right. That's what his name means. Look at the TEETH on him!"

Sammy said, "I thought the 'rex' part was 'wrecks,' because he wrecked other dinosaurs."

Bill said, "I bet that lost kid's day is sure wrecked."

Mrs. Tandy said, "I wonder if we could help find the child?"

Dave said, "Why don't we walk down to the mall office and find out?"

They found the office and Sammy banged on the door.

It opened fast. A huge man stood frowning down at them.

There was a group of men and women in uniform behind him.

The huge man growled, "What do you people want?"

Dave said, "We heard a child was lost. Can we help?"

The man barked, "Come inside."

Then he said, "Are you the ones who MADE that announcement?"

Dave said, "Why are you asking us about your own announcement?"

The man looked slowly at each of them. He calmed down.

He said, "I'm Clint Diego, security chief.

"These are the mall guards.

"A few minutes ago, I locked my office. I went to the dinosaur display to check crowd control. We have to, on opening day.

"While I was out, someone got in here ... and used the loudspeaker.

"The mall guards were called here for nothing.

"I'm sorry I was rude, but there is NO missing child."

Dave looked lost in thought. He said, "Someone went to a lot of trouble for a trick.

"There are some costly antiques here, and a priceless, rare journal, too. Are those things all OK?"

Mr. Diego said, "Yes. The antiques won't be set out until ten.

"And we don't have to worry about the journal ... even though it's worth a huge sum.

"It's in the west end hall, with its own alarm system ... the best that money can buy."

Bill said, "Well, then let's get back to the dinosaurs. Nice meeting you, Mr. Diego."

They hurried toward the Tyrannosaurus rex display.

But when they arrived, Dave said, "Let's go right on through. I want to check something."

He pushed his chair fast, down to the west end display hall.

In the middle of the hall stood a shiny black stand.

Above the stand hung this sign:

EARLY DINOSAUR FOSSIL JOURNAL

On the floor lay a box-like cover made of thick plastic.

Dave shouted, "That's the cover from the display case.

"THE CASE IS EMPTY!   THE JOURNAL IS GONE!"

Chapter 4:
An Electronic Genius

Bill shouted, "I'll go get Mr. Diego!" He took off.

Sammy said, "I'm taking a closer look around here!

"And you don't have to tell me. I won't touch anything."

In front of the display case was a large, square step.

It was screwed to the floor.

Sammy said, "Look, that's for kids to stand on.

"And look, there are screws lying on the floor.

"They must be from the display case lid."

They heard running footsteps. Bill and Mr. Diego rushed in.

Mr. Diego took one look. He turned pale ... for a moment.

Then his color came back and he turned red as a radish.

He gasped, "This system was supposed to be foolproof!

"Only an electronic genius could break into it."

He took out his cell phone, "Guards, cover all doors.

"The journal is gone. Search all packages ... the size of the journal or larger."

Mr. Diego asked the Woodlanders, "Please keep shoppers out of this hall. I'm calling for police backup from nearby towns.

"I'll have to go to my office for the phone numbers."

The family lined up across the opening to the hall. They explained to the other people that the journal display was closed for the time being.

Out-of-town police began pouring into the mall.

Sammy poked Mrs. Tandy and grinned. He said, "LOOK, Mrs. T!

"Chief Hemster is coming. Go hug your best BOYfriend, Mrs. Tandy."

Mrs. Tandy placed a noisy kiss on

Sammy's cheek. "Don't you know that YOU'RE my best boyfriend, Sammy?"

Sammy wiped his face, but he was grinning.

Police Chief Hemster was the Woodland family's best friend.

He smiled and waved and said, "I've got to see Mr. Diego now. The police will take over here.

"Let's meet at the food court upstairs in an hour.

"Then you can tell me everything you know."

Mall guards came down the main hall to the west hall and began looking for clues.

The Woodlanders slowly walked back to the dinosaur exhibit.

First, they looked at a dinosaur with a fancy back.

Mrs. Tandy said, "Look at that Stegosaurus!" She said it like this: steg-uh-SORE-us.

"My lands, his back looks like it has giant teeth sticking up from it."

Bill said, "Hey, would you look at this Triceratops!" It sounded like try-SARE-uh-tops.

"He looks awful ... like a rhino and a lizard, put together."

Just then, SOMETHING GRABBED BILL'S LEG!

"YIKES!" He let out a screech and jumped straight up!

Then he saw Sammy ... with his hand out, ready to pinch again.

Bill said, "Blast it, Sammy, you are a world-class brat. If you were a dinosaur, someone would name you BRATosaurus rex."

Sammy grinned and said, "I was just giving you a free I.Q. test.

"You failed. You thought it was a stegosaurus that bit you."

Bill couldn't help laughing.

Then he said, "Look at that guy working on that bunch of wires.

"And look at that dinosaur. Its side is open. Let's take a look over there."

The wires were fastened to a control panel.

A small young man was hunched over the panel.

He had long, stringy hair and a skinny moustache.

The moustache hung down on each side like two black strings.

And he had a little pointed black beard.

Sammy thought, "He looks like a sneak."

Wires ran from the panel to a motor inside the dinosaur. Rods reached from the motor into the dinosaur's legs and neck.

Four knobs stuck out of a board near the panel.

A large sign over the dinosaur said: MOVE A KNOB. MAKE ME MOVE. PRESS A BUTTON. MAKE ME ROAR.

Mrs. Tandy said, "This looks like fun."

She moved a knob and the dinosaur's neck lifted.

Bill moved another knob and a front leg moved.

Dave said to the man, "This is amazing. Did you do all the wiring?"

Without looking up, the man gave a nervous little smile.

Almost in a whisper, he answered, "I … um … er … and people I trained … did it."

Then he looked back at the wires he was working on.

Bill said, "How did you learn to do this stuff?"

The man didn't seem to want to talk. In a low voice, he said, "Well ... um ... in school ... and from other people."

Mrs. Tandy said, "Well, you're an electronic genius!"

The man smiled a little and went back to his work.

Suddenly, Sammy looked wild-eyed. He poked Bill and whispered, "He's an electronic genius, Bill! Think about that!

"I bet he knows more about wiring than anyone else here. Enough to take a security system apart."

"And look at that moustache. I bet it's fake. When he takes it off, no one could even remember what he looked like with it.

"I bet the thief of that journal is standing RIGHT IN FRONT OF US WIRING
THAT PANEL!"

Chapter 5:
The Clue

Bill grabbed Sammy's arm.

He pulled him away from the open dinosaur.

He dragged him halfway around the display hall.

Then he said, "For crying out loud, Sammy, he might have heard what you said!

"Just because he's good with electricity and machines doesn't mean he's the thief."

Sammy said, "Get your big paws off me you ... you ... JERKasaurus! I'm going to watch that guy.

"I'm going to FIND some proof, because I know I'm right!"

He darted away from Bill.

He went back to where the dinosaur man was working.

He whispered to Dave, "You guys go and meet Chief Hemster without me. I'm setting up a stakeout on this guy."

Dave whispered back, "A stakeout? Why?"

Sammy said, "Because he's the thief who took that journal, that's why.

"Did you notice how he doesn't want to talk to anyone?

"And when he does talk, he whispers ... to get rid of you!

"And he doesn't look you in the eye!

"Did you notice that moustache? I bet it's a fake.

"And that stupid beard. The end even comes to a point ... like a bad guy's in a movie.

"All you have to do is look at him to know he's guilty!

"And besides, he knows everything about wiring."

Bill followed Sammy. He whispered, "Listen here, Sammy. Don't you remember the first rule of U.S. law?

"A person is innocent until proven guilty."

Sammy said, "So? I'll prove he's guilty!

"He probably even hid the journal inside a dinosaur."

Just then, Kathy picked up something from the floor.

Sammy said, "What did you find, Kathy? Let us see it."

Kathy said, "It's just a business card, Sammy.

"It's so dirty ... a million people must have stepped on it."

She handed it to Dave.

Dave handed the card around to the others.

This is what they saw:

JAMES OLSON
BOOKSELLER'S ALLEY

•*Rare books* •*Everyday books* •*Books to bring joy to every heart*
•*Comfortable chairs* •*Come to buy, or just to read*

In back of

135 South San Domingo St.
Miller Town
Phone 555-1234

Dave said, "Miller Town isn't more than ten miles from home. Let's go sometime."

Mrs. Tandy said, "SOMETIME ends up being NO TIME.

"Why don't we spend this afternoon there?

"I love good mysteries. I might find one there."

Kathy said, "It sounds good to me, too.

"Maybe they have books about careers in medicine. That's what I want to find out about."

Dave said, "Maybe they have books about finishing wood. I'm going to build a bookcase in shop."

Bill said, "Well, to tell the truth, I'll be glad to get out of here. A little mall goes a long way with me.

"After a while you realize it's not a great place to do things ... just a place to buy things."

But Sammy said, "Leave the mall? Not on your life! You're not going to

44

drag me away.

"I'm going to be on my stake out, watching that guy!

"Come back and get me when the mall closes."

Bill said, "Gee, too bad, Sammy. No bookstore. And no lunch with Chief Hemster. Well, come on everyone, time to eat.

"Good-bye, Sammy. See you tonight, when the mall closes." He turned and walked away.

Sammy took a last look at the dinosaur man.

Then he turned and darted after Bill and the others.

Mrs. Tandy said, "Why are you so quiet, Dave?"

Dave said, "I was just thinking. What if Kathy HAS found a clue?

"After all, just a few minutes after a

terribly rare book is stolen ... she found
a card from a RARE BOOK STORE!"

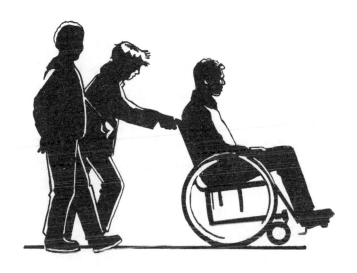

Chapter 6:
Bookstore, Here We Come

They walked past table after table in the halls.

The antique dealers had just set up.

"Who would have thought lizards could get so big?" Sammy said.

Dave said, "Dinosaurs aren't really lizards, even though the word 'dinosaur' means 'terrible lizard.' They're more like birds. In fact, birds are their closest relatives."

Sammy laughed. "Sure, Dave! And I suppose old Tyrannosaurus rex could fly, too!"

Chief Hemster was waiting for them at the food court.

He had a cup of coffee and a BIG sweet roll.

He saw the Woodlanders coming. He cut the roll into six pieces.

He said, "You got here in the nick of time!

"You saved me from eating this thing by myself."

Sammy said, "I'm hungry as a wolf!" and gobbled his piece down.

The chief said, "Go pick out what food

you want.

"I'll follow you around. Lunch is on me.

"And hurry up, everyone. We have to talk about this case."

In a few minutes, they sat down together.

Dave said, "Chief, take a look at this card. Kathy found it on the floor at the dinosaur display.

"It's from a store that buys and sells rare books. Does that seem strange to you ... to find it the day that journal disappeared?"

The chief looked at it. He said, "It IS strange. It might be a clue ... our only clue.

"What else do we have to go on? The guards saw the journal in the case at nine.

"So the theft had to happen after nine.

"And before ten-fifteen ... when you all saw the journal was missing.

"There were sixty-five people at work in the mall before ten ...

for security

cleaning

food service

repairs

... and to work on the dinosaurs.

"The antique dealers weren't walking around at ten.

"The stores' salespeople were told to stay inside the shops.

"If the theft happened before ten, it's likely a mall worker did it.

"Later, any one of thousands could have done it."

Bill said, "Well, no matter WHO, there's still the question of HOW."

Kathy swallowed a bite of sweet roll and said, "We think it happened right

after that fake loudspeaker message. That was right at ten."

"How could anyone unlock the office ...
use the loudspeaker
run to the end of the mall
stop the electronic system
un-screw the display case
grab the book

... and get it outside, all in less than fifteen minutes?"

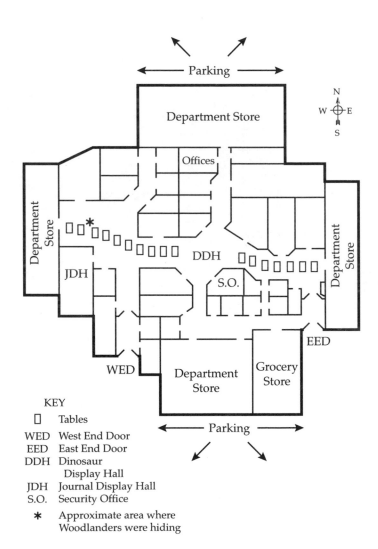

KEY

☐   Tables
WED   West End Door
EED   East End Door
DDH   Dinosaur
        Display Hall
JDH   Journal Display Hall
S.O.   Security Office

∗   Approximate area where
    Woodlanders were hiding

Chief Hemster said, "If it was a mall-worker, it isn't in his or her car. The police asked the workers if we could search their cars.

"Every single one said yes. We found nothing."

Dave said, "Then the journal might still be here, hidden in the mall ... even if two people pulled this off, working together."

Bill said, "Let's say the thief IS someone who works here. Then he or she would probably know a lot of good hiding places."

Up till now, Sammy had been munching a hamburger and slurping milk.

Now he came up for air. He said, "Listen, Chief. I already KNOW who the thief is, but Bill won't listen to me.

"It's the dinosaur man. He did it. Just look at the facts."

Sammy told the chief what he had told Bill.

He added, "And besides, the book store card was on the floor in front of his display.

"He's guilty, all right. I know about these things."

Bill put down his pizza slice.

He said, "Come on, Sammy. Don't be

silly. If he stole the journal, where is it? Do you know about THAT thing, too?"

Kathy said, "This mall's big.

"There are a million places to hide even a BIG book."

Sammy said, "Listen I bet I DO know where that journal is. Inside that open dinosaur!

"I bet you ANYthing, and I'm going to look in there."

He darted away, like a lizard after a bug.

In a couple of minutes, he came back looking glum.

He said, "Here's how sly that dinosaur man is. As soon as I asked, he let me look inside ... because he KNEW the journal wasn't there.

"But that doesn't mean he DIDN'T steal it.

"He's just hidden it some other place.

"So let's go down to Bookseller's Alley. That's probably where he plans to sell it.

"The bookstore owner's probably a criminal, too.

"I can see him in my mind. A tall, sneaky, man ... with a twisted mouth. And shifty eyes that flit from side to side.

"We can go right now and check him out for you, Chief!"

Chief Hemster said, "That's not a bad idea, Sammy.

"But don't say anything to bother him. Chances are, he isn't guilty of a thing.

"But maybe you CAN discover something that might help.

"Go for it, all of you. And I'll meet you for dinner tonight."

Chapter 7:
Inside the Green Door

Outside the mall, the family began to RUN in the icy wind.

They pushed Dave so fast he shouted, "Slow down!

"What do you think this is, a dogsled race?"

Sammy panted, "We can't stop. We'd freeze into statues."

But they warmed up as they drove to Miller Town.

They got out and the icy wind caught them again.

Bill said, "Are you sure this is the right alley, Dave? It's jammed with trucks."

Sammy said, "It looks like truck heaven. Watch out, Mrs. Tandy. That one's backing up!"

Kathy pointed to a brick wall with books painted on it.

There was a green door in the wall. Above it was written

BOOK SELLER'S ALLEY.

They hurried inside. The store was cozy and bright.

Books lined every wall.

Wooden box-like steps lay in front of some shelves.

The steps reminded Dave of the one in front of the rare journal display ... at the mall.

Mrs. Tandy said, "It smells a bit like cinnamon in here."

They all loved the store ... except Sammy, that is.

His eyes were darting around ... and his forehead was wrinkled.

Bill poked Dave with his elbow.

He whispered, "Look at Sammy. He looks like a bloodhound sniffing out a killer."

A man was standing at the far end of the room.

He was holding a book. He smiled and called, "Welcome!"

Sammy forgot what Chief Hemster had said about being polite. He barked,

"Where's the owner?"

The man answered politely, "I'm the owner, James Olson.

"You've saved me from a lonesome day. Not many people come out in this bitter weather.

"All the shelves are marked. You will be able to find whatever books you want.

"Now, some of my shelves are very high.

"Move the box steps to where you need them. They're hollow, so they're not heavy.

"But don't move this one. I've stored some books under it."

He walked back to where he had been working.

Bill poked Sammy's arm and whispered, "I thought you said he'd be a mean guy. Tall. Sneaky. With a twisty mouth.

"Not a bad guess ... except he's nice. And he's middle-sized, not tall.

"And he's not sneaky. And his mouth isn't twisty.

"Sure doesn't look like a criminal to me."

Sammy whispered, "Well, I guess maybe looks don't tell everything, after all.

"So what if the man does look OK? This PLACE doesn't look OK.

"A truck could un-load right at the door. That's why the store's in this alley.

"He probably buys truck loads of stolen books."

Sammy trotted straight to the back of the room.

They heard him call, "There's another room back here, and it's HUGE."

Mr. Olson called to him, "There are three more rooms, too. Keep walking and you'll see them all.

"Lucky for me my son helps out. He makes plastic covers for the rare books.

"And he knows as much about books as I do.

"He's here evenings, and sometimes on weekends. Today, he's busy and I'm alone.

"But call me if you have questions.

And help yourselves to some candy."

CANDY! The magic word. Sammy looked around.

AND SUDDENLY HE SAW CANDY.

A bowl of buttermints here.

A jar of gumdrops there.

A dish of jelly beans across the room.

He raced to each table. He stuffed gumdrops into one pocket.

He stuffed a handful of jelly beans into another.

He stuffed a handful of buttermints into his mouth.

Suddenly, Bill came into the room.

He said, "Sammy! Mr. Olson said, 'Take a candy.' He didn't say take a carload.

"Talk about a thief!"

Sammy said, "That's all YOU know, Billy big-mouth. I was getting candy for all of us. And that's the thanks I get."

Sammy's mouth was so stuffed, Bill could hardly understand him.

Bill said, "Oh, so the candies are for all of us. I see you were carrying them in your MOUTH for us. Yum, yum."

He began to laugh.

Sammy didn't want Bill to see how stuffed-full his mouth was. So he put his hand in front of it.

Then he couldn't help it. He began to laugh too.

Out shot the whole mouthful of juicy mints ... all over the palm of his hand!

Chapter 8:
The Back Room

Bill said, "Sammy!

"Wait here!

"And don't touch a single book ... or ANYthing!"

He rushed to find Mr. Olson. He said, "Quick, Mr. Olson. Sammy's got his hands sticky.

"Is there a place where he can wash up?"

Mr. Olson laughed and said, "I bet I know what happened.

"Once in a while the candy seems too good, even to me.

"Come on in, I'll take you folks back to my workroom."

Sammy whispered to Bill, "I heard that. Maybe it's the place where he does his crimes! Now I can look for proof."

Bill whispered, "Listen, Sammy, you're going too far about this book business!"

That made Sammy mad. He waved his sticky hand near Bill's face.

Bill jumped away.

Sammy laughed and said, "Ha! I wasn't really going to touch you!"

The family followed Mr. Olson into a small room.

At first, they couldn't see anything in it.

Sammy whispered, "See how dark he keeps it in here? He's afraid we will see too much."

But Mr. Olson turned a switch ... and the room became light as day.

What did they see?

Books. Books on the floor. Books on top of each other.

Piles of books that were taller than Kathy.

Sammy said, "Wow, it's a CITY of books."

Mr. Olson said, "More like a mountain ... a mountain of work.

"I have to find out about each book before I put it on a shelf. But it's work that I love doing.

"I sort the books into different piles over here."

"Rare books ... such as diaries and rare journals ... are on that table ... against the wall."

Sammy gasped when he heard the words "rare journals." Bill poked him to keep him quiet. He said, "Oops! Sorry, Sammy."

Mr. Olson led them to a sink. "Here's

soap and a towel."

Sammy said, "This'll take me a pretty long time.

"Why don't you go on with what you were doing, Mr. Olson?

"We can turn off the light when I'm cleaned up."

Mr. Olson said, "Look around at these books if you'd like.

"You can handle them, but not the rare books against this wall.

"And please don't touch that table. Those are my son's books."

While Sammy washed up he growled, "Rotten rats!

"I thought I'd trap him when I said he should leave us here.

"I thought that he had hidden the missing journal with his other rare journals.

"I thought he wouldn't give us a

chance to be here alone."

Bill said, "Doesn't this prove something, Sammy? Doesn't this show he's not a criminal?"

Sammy had a stubborn-as-a-mule look on his face.

He said, "No, it just proves that he's clever. He's hidden away the stolen stuff. So he isn't afraid we will find it.

"Look, there's even a back door in this room ... so he can escape if the police come!"

Bill laughed and said, "Get real, Sammy. EVERY business has to have a back door. It's part of the fire safety code.

"Now, take a look around and let's get out of here."

Dave said, "What luck. Here we are, five book lovers in a room full of books. I feel like a pig loose in a garden!"

He wheeled over to the piles of rare books along the wall.

He read a title out loud, "*Dorothy and the Wizard in Oz.*"

Sammy said, "*Dorothy and the Wizard in OZ!* A rare book?

"Ha! He doesn't know a thing about books.

"That's not rare. You can get a copy

71

of it when ever you want. At any school or library.

"I've read it three times already my self."

Dave said, "But not THIS copy, Sammy. It's a first printing, and it is old and rare."

Sammy looked at all the piles of books. He even lay down to look at ones near the floor.

Bill said, "Books from the olden days have such nice bindings. They were made to last."

Mrs. Tandy said, "What do you mean, 'olden days'?

"Some of these look like books I owned when I was little!

"Am I just a leftover from the olden days?"

Bill said, "Oh, no, Mrs. T. I'm sorry if I hurt your feelings. I wouldn't do that for the world."

Mrs. Tandy hugged him. She said, "I was just teasing you, Bill."

By then, Sammy was done snooping. He said, "Well, I don't see any clues in here."

Then he passed near the books that belonged to Mr. Olson's son.

He stopped in front of them and shouted, "Wow! You'll HAVE to believe me now!"

Chapter 9:
Waiting

Sammy covered his mouth.

He said, "Oops! I hope Mr. Olson didn't hear me.

"Quick, come look at these books. But don't make any noise."

The family crowded around.

Dave whispered as he read the titles out loud, "*Electric Wiring ... Modern Electrical Methods ...* "

Sammy broke in, "Listen to this one: *Electricity from A to Z, Alarm Systems to Zoom Cameras.*"

Bill said, "Wow, Sammy! These books COULD belong to a thief ... one who wanted to break into an alarm system."

Mrs. Tandy said, "Good heavens! Mr. Olson said they're his SON'S books! That might mean it was his son who stole the journal."

Sammy said, "This PROVES it! Mr. Olson is a criminal, too!"

Dave said, "Wait a minute, you two. Just wait a minute.

"What about a person being innocent until PROVEN guilty?"

Bill said, "Oops, we got carried away.

"First, we thought the dinosaur man might be the thief.

"Now we say Mr. Olson's son is guilty.

"And all we have are some books about electricity ... but not a bit of real proof."

Sammy said, "Well, that's MY proof."

Kathy said, "I think we ought to go talk to Chief Hemster."

Sammy said, "Well, I'm not leaving this store yet. I'm going to see that son first.

"Mr. Olson said he was coming here after work. I want to see if he walks in with a package that could be that journal."

"And you guys have to stay here with me. Remember, I'm still the boss for today."

Bill said, "To tell the truth, I want to

stay. I'd like to get a look at Mr. Olson's son."

The others felt the same way.

Dave said, "Let's get out of this workroom. We don't want Mr. Olson to know what we think.

"Let's start looking at books in the big rooms.

"It's four now. His son might work until five … and come in by five-thirty."

Mrs. Tandy said, "Well, I'm going to look at mystery novels."

Dave said, "I'll stay in the second room with the history books. Each person take a room.

"That way we can keep watch after his son comes in. One of us would always be near him."

Sammy said, "I have dibs on the room next to the workroom.

"I don't care WHAT books I look

at there.

"I just want to hear if he comes into the workroom from outside."

But in a while Sammy appeared in Bill's room.

Bill said, "Hi, Sammy. What's the problem? Do you want to trade rooms?"

Sammy said, "No, I don't want to trade.

"I've got the best room in the whole store.

"My books have wonderful printing in them. Some have fancy old-fashioned letters.

"Some of their pages are thick paper, almost like cloth.

"And the chairs in there are big and soft. I love my room."

Bill said, "Well then, why did you come in here?"

Sammy said, "HERE'S why!"

He darted over to a bowl of candy on the table next to Bill.

It was full of brightly wrapped chocolates.

He grabbed the whole bowl. He raced back to his room with it.

He called, "Thanks," and disappeared.

Every once in a while, Mr. Olson walked into his workroom ... to take a few books to the front.

At 5:20 P.M., Mrs. Tandy heard a voice call from outside, "Here I am, Dad, and I've got it."

She rushed to get the kids, but Sammy was missing.

Then Bill had an idea. He found Sammy in the work room. He was hiding under the table near the door, eating chocolates.

Sammy whispered, "I'm waiting for his son in here.

"I'm SURE he will sneak in through the back door!"

Bill said, "Come on, Sammy. He's already inside the store!

"And he carried in a big box. It's on the front table!

"And you'll never guess in a million years who Mr. Olson's son is!"

Chapter 10:
What's in the Box?

The family went to the front of the store ... and stopped dead.

Who was standing next to Mr. Olson? The electronic genius dinosaur man!

They heard him say, "I hope I got what you wanted, Dad."

Then he noticed the Woodlanders.

Almost in a whisper he said, "H- H- Hello."

Then he didn't say another word to anyone.

Dave was the first to get over his surprise.

He said, "Oh, uh, hello.

"We found a card from your father's shop. So we came to see what the shop was like."

Mr. Olson said, "This is my son, Charles Olson, Junior."

Dave said, "Nice to meet you. But we have to go now."

Bill hurried over to a couch where they'd left their coats.

Then he grabbed Sammy and pushed him out the front door.

Sammy said, "Wait a minute! I'm not done here yet!

"I want to find out just what's in that b … ."

Bill clapped a hand over Sammy's mouth.

That made Sammy MAD! He stuck his tongue out as he wiggled loose.

He said, "Keep your big hand off my mouth!"

"I was going to make them tell us what was in that box!"

Bill said, "I know, and I kept you from making a BIG mistake with your BIG mouth."

Just then the others came out of the book shop door.

Mrs. Tandy said, "Wow, that was a close call.

"Sammy, I'm so proud of you. You didn't give us away.

"I was afraid you'd try to make them open that box.

"If it was the journal, they'd never have shown us.

"And we'd have spoiled things for the police."

Sammy gave Bill a begging look. He said, "I wouldn't do that. I'm not a dumb bunny, you know."

Bill kept his mouth shut, but he wore a big grin.

Kathy said, "You know what Dave did after you boys went out? It was so brave!

"When he was putting on his coat, he let his arm slip ... on purpose. He shot his hand through the sleeve and hit the box!

"And guess what? It slid right across the desk.

"The box was light. It wasn't a book at all."

Dave said, "I told them I was sorry I bumped it. And Mr. Olson said, 'That's OK.

"'It's just take-out chicken and cole slaw ... and a dozen sweet rolls. Charlie stops for our dinner on the way home.'"

"Boy, did I feel foolish," Dave added.

Sammy said, "Well, I don't. I still think I'm right. Young Charlie Olson stole that journal, and I'm going to prove it!"

Bill said, "OK, Mr. Right, get into the car.

"We've got to go tell Chief Hemster what we know."

They piled in. As he drove Dave said, "But what do we really know?

"Just that the dinosaur man studies

electronics. And he needs to do that for his work.

"And we know his dad is a nice guy who owns a bookstore. That doesn't mean his dad sells stolen books."

Bill said, "You're right I suppose, Dave. But still ... ."

Mrs. Tandy said, "Well, we've got another important mystery to solve.

"What are we having for dinner? It's Dave and Kathy's turn to cook.

"But we won't be home in time for you two to do any fancy cooking."

Sammy said, "I can solve this mystery easily. Let's take out that big roasting pan. The one in the basement freezer.

"It's full of pot roast and carrots and onions and potatoes. And they're already cooked.

"We can be home by ten of six. I bet you can heat it up by seven-thirty. The chief won't mind waiting for pot roast."

But the way things turned out, the chief didn't have to wait at all. They had to wait for him.

He didn't get to the house until almost 8:00 P.M.

He said, "I'm sorry to be this late."

Bill said, "That's all right. Now sit down. Do WE have things to tell YOU!"

Sammy said, "You know that dinosaur guy?

"Well, his name is Olson, Charles Olson, Junior.

"And you won't believe this. He's ... ."

Chief Hemster said, "You Woodlanders! We can't fool you. How in the world did you find out ... that he's working with the F.B.I.?"

Chapter 11:
We Know Who Stole It

Bill gasped. "The dinosaur man is working with the F.B.I.?"

Sammy stared in surprise. His mouth
hung wide open.

He said, "I thought he STOLE the book. I sure didn't think he was helping FIND the missing journal.

"He looks so guilty!"

The chief said, "Sammy, have you ever heard the saying, 'You can't judge a book by its cover'?

"Well, that means you can't tell anything about a person just from the way he or she looks.

"Charlie Olson is just a very shy person.

"When he talks to anyone he doesn't know, he stutters.

"He's OK with his family, but he can't look a stranger in the eye without stuttering.

"Yet, he is a real genius with electronics.

"Charlie's one book you can't tell by its cover."

Mrs. Tandy said, "Well, John, I can tell what YOU'RE like from the way you look. HUNGRY.

"So let's eat. We can talk afterward."

At first, there was no talking ... just munching.

Then Dave said, "Tell us, Chief, how did you learn that Charles Olson was helping?"

Chief Hemster said, "An F.B.I. agent turned up.

"She filled us in on another crime ... one that took place seven months ago.

"A jewelry store in another mall had a display of precious jewels on loan from a museum. The store was robbed clean."

Dave said, "But how does Charlie fit into the picture?

The chief explained, "A dinosaur display was going on in that other mall, too.

"The police called in the F.B.I. The F.B.I. questioned every worker there.

"They began to suspect Charlie's helpers. But they didn't have proof.

"Charlie's worked with the F.B.I. ever since.

"He's set up displays at several malls since then. The same helpers have been with him."

Mrs. Tandy said, "It must have been hard on him. He had to act as if nothing were wrong."

The chief said, "He kept close watch, but nothing happened ... until today.

"Today, he struck pay dirt."

Sammy said, "There's MY pay dirt!"

He stabbed a brown potato with his fork. Gravy splashed up onto Mrs. Tandy's sleeve.

"Oops, gee, I'm really sorry, Mrs. Tandy."

Mrs. Tandy said, "Your pay dirt was more like SPRAY dirt. But it's no big deal. A little water will take it off."

Dave asked, "What pay dirt did Charlie Olson find, Chief?"

The chief said, "This morning, before ten, he spotted one of the men sneaking down the hall toward the front office.

"Charlie's been carrying a tiny camera. It prints the time and date of a picture on the film.

"He snapped a picture of the man picking the office lock ... and entering the office."

Bill asked, "How come he didn't call the F.B.I. right then?"

Chief Hemster said, "He got worried about the journal.

"He rushed back down the hall.

"And sure enough, there was the OTHER man he suspected fooling with the alarm control box."

Dave said, "Did he get HIS picture, too?"

The chief said, "Just one before the fellow began to look around. So Charlie

had to duck and hide. A minute later he ran back to the display, but the journal was gone."

Mrs. Tandy said, "So now the thieves are under arrest, right?"

Chief Hemster said, "Wrong."

Sammy said, "Then what are we sitting here for?

"Let's get back to the mall. Let's arrest those guys!"

He jumped up from his chair.

He raced to the closet for his coat and hat.

Chief Hemster called after him, "Whoa! Hold your horses!

"It's Saturday night.   The mall is closed."

Sammy roared, "Closed! And I just bet they sneaked the book out before closing time.

"Now you'll NEVER get it back, Chief."

Chief Hemster said, "Listen, Sammy. We didn't even let them know we had their pictures.   We don't want to scare them away.

"Because we think the journal is STILL IN THE MALL!

"We checked every package that went out today. We found NOTHING.

"At closing time, we searched every store and locked it.

"We know HOW that rare journal was stolen.

"And we know WHO stole it.

"But we don't know WHERE IT'S HID-DEN.

"Except that it's someplace in that mall!"

Sammy said, "So why wait?

"Let's go open the mall. Let's go find that book! Right now! Tonight!"

Chapter 12:
The Big Book Hunt

Chief Hemster said, "I think that's a great idea.

"We WERE going to start again at six tomorrow morning. But I'm all for beginning right now.

"You kids snoop better than a pack of bloodhounds.

"I'll phone Mr. Diego. He can tell the F.B.I. what our plan is."

When he was done on the phone, the chief said, "He wants to meet us there."

Dave said, "Everyone bundle up! It's even colder now."

They put on every sweater that would fit inside their coats.

They put on gloves and scarves and earmuffs and boots.

Mrs. Tandy said, "We look like big stuffed toys."

Sammy saw Mrs. Tandy's red wool cape. He threw it on and ran around yelling, "Super Snoop to the rescue!"

Then Sammy tripped and fell on his stomach. But he was wearing so many clothes, he wasn't hurt. It was like falling onto a mattress.

Mrs. Tandy said, "Give me my cape, you scamp.

"Maybe try that big, woolen skating sweater over your jacket. It's thicker than my cape, and it won't trip you up."

Sammy was so packed in, he couldn't bend his arms.

■   ■   ■

The mall was almost dark. Only a few dim, ghostly lights were on.

Mr. Diego greeted them inside the door at the east end.

He said, "Be careful not to bump into anything. Tables of antiques are everywhere.

"Suppose we start down at the other end.

"We can work our way back to this end, where we've parked."

They left their outer clothes in piles at the east end.

Mr. Diego unlocked a big metal panel in his office. It was full of electric switches. He turned on the lights they'd need first.

Chief Hemster said, "Let's see. All the stores have been searched and locked. What other places do you think we should search?"

Mr. Diego said, "Well, the cleaning supply rooms."

Sammy said, "I'll help with those. I want to find out what you keep in them."

Chief Hemster said, "Becky, why don't you and Kathy check out all the women's bathrooms?

"Dave and I will check out the men's rooms."

Mr. Diego said, "Bill and I can check the offices ... and the rooms where we do repairs.

"If you notice any cupboards, I have keys to open them all.

"But the big job will be searching all those tables of antiques."

Mr. Diego took a folded paper from his pocket. He said, "I brought this to show you the size of the missing book."

He unfolded it. It was three times as big as a regular book page.

"Wow," Sammy said. "It's as big as a photo album. That's one big journal."

Mr. Diego said, "The book is so big because it was used as both a journal and a sketchbook.

"In those days, people didn't have cameras. When a fossil hunter found new sites, he would sketch out everything in the landscape before he began to dig. That way people would know where fossils came from."

Then Mr. Diego took a short ladder out of his office. He said, "This is for looking on top of anything too high."

So the search began. They combed the journal display hall, but found nothing.

They looked under the plastic sheets covering the antiques.

Then they started pulling out boxes from under the tables.

Dave said, "A book could even be hanging below, tied to the bottom of the table by ropes."

They searched every cupboard and closet and cabinet top.

Hour after hour, they searched. They hardly talked.

The only sounds were made by boxes scraping over the floor.

Sammy said, "Boy, it's so creepy in here at night. But it doesn't scare me."

Just the same, he stuck close to Bill.

At last, they came to the dinosaur hall.

They looked at every part of each animal.

They searched all the plastic bushes and trees around them.

They looked through the live flowers growing in the mall planters.

By twelve midnight, they had searched everywhere, upstairs and down.

They were back near the door they had come in.

They had not found the journal.

Sadly, Chief Hemster said, "Well, I guess that's it. I only hope tomorrow we come up with something we've missed today."

Mr. Diego turned off the bright lights. Only the dim nighttime lights were on.

They began putting on their outer clothes.

Bill dressed the fastest. Finally, he had on so much, he felt hot.

That's why he was in the outer hall ... looking out toward the parking lot.

Suddenly, he darted back in.

He said, "Hold it, everybody! Don't fin-
ish dressing!

"A black car just pulled into the lot.
It had its headlights off.

"I just happened to see a piece of its
shiny trim.

"It drove way down, to the west end
of the mall."

Kathy said, "Who'd be coming out here at this time of night?"

Chief Hemster said, "Let's find out. Stick close to us, Woodlanders. Don't make a sound. Follow us down to the other end."

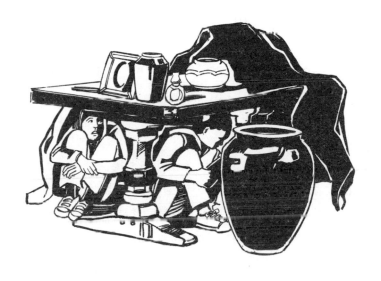

Chapter 13:
Shadows in the Moonlight

They found that the display tables were perfect to hide under.

Dave whispered to the family, "Stay down low.

"And try not to bump the plastic. It's noisy."

Like shadows in moonlight, they slipped along.

They finally stopped near the west end of the mall.

To the left, they could see a door to the parking lot. Straight ahead, they could look into the journal display hall.

In a moment, they heard the outside door open. Two men sneaked inside.

Chief Hemster whispered, "It's Charlie's helpers!"

Bill whispered, "I bet they'll lead us straight to the journal!"

But suddenly lights shined in from the lot. A car door slammed.

The two men turned. They ran past the table where Chief Hemster was hiding.

The chief stood up and called, "Stop ... Stay right where you are!"

For one second, the men stood as still as stones.

Then they ran across the hall in the dim light.

They passed near the table where Sammy and Bill were hiding.

Sammy jumped up. He screamed his most horrible scream.

He waved his arms in front of the men.

The men stopped running and froze.

Chief Hemster ran over and clamped handcuffs onto the two men.

Then a woman walked in from the cold. Mr. Diego called to her, "Why, Jan. I thought you weren't coming until morning."

It was Janet Short, the F.B.I. agent. She said, "I decided to see how you were doing."

She looked around. She said, "Why, those are the suspects!"

The chief said, "We think they were coming to get the journal.

"But they started running the minute they saw your lights."

One of the men said, "We don't know anything about a journal."

The other one said, "Yeah, we were just coming in to work on the dinosaurs.

"You can't charge us with anything."

Chief Hemster said, "How about breaking and entering?"

Kathy said, "If you're here to check on the dinosaurs ... why didn't you park near the middle door, closer to the dinosaur display?

"I bet you the book's hidden in the journal display hall!"

Sammy groaned, "Don't be silly, Kathy. We searched every inch of it. We didn't find a single thing in there.

"And I'm hot, and it's late, and I'm tired.

"And I want to sit down."

The only thing to sit on was the big wooden step ... the one in front of the empty display case.

So Sammy walked over and sat down on it. He kept right on complaining.

"It's too bad Agent Short drove up when she did.

"We were just getting to the seat of the trouble. Now we might never get to the end of it."

At those words, Dave said, "SEAT of the trouble! END!

"Hey, I think I know where the journal is!

"Sammy, you're sitting on top of the seat of the trouble!"

He pointed to the wooden step under Sammy. "Remember the books stored under a step at Mr. Olson's bookstore?

"I bet THIS step's hollow too ... just like his, only this one's screwed to the floor.

"Remember the screws we saw on the floor this morning? Well, we thought they came from the journal display case lid.

"But I think one of them came from this step ... when they un-screwed it to hide the journal. See, there's a screw missing."

Sammy took out his pocketknife.

He opened the screwdriver and un-screwed the step.

Slowly and carefully, Mr. Diego lifted it up.

There lay the missing journal.

■   ■   ■

At ten o'clock Sunday morning, the Woodlanders gave a brunch.

Their guests were Chief Hemster, Agent Short, Mr. Diego, and the Olsons.

For dessert, Sammy brought in a big platter of cookies.

He said, "I made these for you, Charlie. I feel bad, because I decided you were a crook ... and I didn't have one bit of proof."

Charlie said, "I'll forgive you, Sammy ... if you'll just hand me some of those cookies."

Sammy passed the platter.

It was loaded with sugar cookies shaped like dinosaurs ... well, like dinosaur bodies.

Most of the heads had broken off their skinny necks.

Sammy said, "They got wrecked when I took them off the cookie sheets.

"They're Tyrannosaurus WRECKS, get it?

"Not R ... E ... X!

"They're W ... R ... E ... C ... K ... S!"

Everyone groaned and then began to laugh. They sat laughing and talking till the cookies were all gone.

And Charlie Olson, Junior, the very shy dinosaur man, ate and talked and laughed as much as anyone else at the party.